Barbie™

Fairytopia™

A Junior Novelization

Adapted by Tisha Hamilton

Based on the screenplay by
Elise Allen, Diane Duane

SCHOLASTIC INC.

New York Toronto London Auckland Sydney
Mexico City New Delhi Hong Kong Buenos Aires

No part of this publication may be reproduced in whole or in part,
or stored in a retrieval system, or transmitted in any form or by any means,
electronic, mechanical, photocopying, recording, or otherwise,
without written permission of the copyright owner.

ISBN 0-439-74086-X

BARBIE and associated trademarks and trade dress are
owned by and used under license from Mattel, Inc.
Copyright © 2005 Mattel, Inc. All Rights Reserved.

Special thanks to: Rob Hudnut, Nancy Bennett, Tiffany J. Shuttleworth,
Rick Rivezzo, Zoë Chance, Vicki Jaeger, Monica Lopez,
Phil Mendoza and Mainframe Entertainment.

Photography by the Mattel Photo Studio.
Book design by Bethany Dixon.

Published by Scholastic Inc.
SCHOLASTIC and associated logos are trademarks and/or
registered trademarks of Scholastic Inc.

12 11 10 9 8 7 6 5 4 3 2 5 6 7 8 9/0

Printed in the U.S.A.
First printing, March 2005

Introduction

Just beyond the rainbow from the world we know lies Fairytopia, a magical place. Fun-loving fairies flutter and glimmer above lush meadows. Mischievous pixies zip and dart in the sparkling sun. Fantastic flowers fill the air with heavenly scents and color the landscape with their pretty hues.

The wise and kind Enchantress watches

over Fairytopia. She is helped by the seven Guardian Fairies, each named for the color of the magical jewel that they wear.

Fairytopia, in fact, is just what it sounds like: a *utopia*, or perfect place, for fairies

and other magic folk. Even little Elina, the wingless fairy who couldn't fly like all the other fairies, was happy in Fairytopia. But all that was about to change. . . .

Chapter 1
Something's Wrong in the Magic Meadow!

Elina peeped out from under a giant flower in the Magic Meadow. The little fairy was playing hide-and-seek with her best friend, Dandelion. She didn't know Dandelion was right behind her. Dandelion hadn't known it, either.

"Eek!" Elina cried in surprise as they both turned to face each other at the same time.

Dandelion giggled. She waited a moment, admiring the beautiful rainbow that shone in Elina's eyes. Then, with a flick of her wings, she zoomed off above the meadow.

Elina took off running right after her. Without wings, she couldn't fly, but she managed to stay right behind Dandelion. They came to a stop when a group of fairies called to Dandelion from high above them.

"I'll be right back," Dandelion said.

Elina watched her fly toward the fairies, feeling disappointed—a familiar sensation. How Elina wished she could fly, too! Why couldn't she be like everyone else?

Elina's puffball, Bibble, floated up to her. She always seemed to know how Elina felt.

Now Bibble snuggled close and purred.

Sneering laughter rang out. It was a group of mean pixies.

Elina tried to ignore them.

"Hey!" one pixie cried. "What do you call a fairy without wings?"

"I don't know," another pixie answered. "What?"

"Nothing!" the first pixie shouted. "Who'd want to call a wingless fairy?"

The pixies tumbled about in the air, laughing themselves silly at their nasty joke.

Bibble trilled with anger, but Elina tried to calm her down. "Don't even bother with them," she said. "They're not worth it."

"Oof!" A sudden gust sent the pixies soaring through the air. Elina looked around and realized it was Dandelion. Her friend had seen the pixies teasing Elina and had flown to her rescue, furiously flapping her wings to blow the pixies away.

"Thanks, Dandelion," Elina said. "What did those fairies want, anyway?"

Dandelion wrinkled her nose. "It was weird," she told Elina. "They said we should go home right away because something bad is happening in the Magic Meadow."

Uneasily, the fairies looked around at their beautiful meadow. It did seem kind of quiet. Suddenly, the tiny swarm of pixies swooped over to them again.

"Back for more?" Dandelion asked, waving her wings.

"Hell-o! We're trying to help you!" snapped one of the pixies. "But hey, if you don't care that somebody kidnapped Topaz, fine!"

"Kidnapped?" Elina gasped. "Topaz, the Guardian Fairy of the Magic Meadow?"

"Well, *duh,* how many Topazes do you know?" the pixie shot back.

"What about the other Guardian Fairies?" asked Dandelion.

"Please! Do we look like we've been all over Fairytopia checking on the other Guardian Fairies?" demanded the pixie.

"But . . . why are you telling us this?" asked

Dandelion. "It's almost . . . nice."

"Just because we make fun of you doesn't mean we want to see you kidnapped by Laverna," the pixie replied.

"Laverna? The evil twin sister of the Enchantress?" scoffed Elina. "She's just a scary story. She doesn't really exist!"

"What-*ever*! *We're* going home where it's *safe*," the pixie huffed, and with that, they all buzzed off.

"*Bleeble broop wallabree?*" chirped Bibble.

"I don't know what that was all about, Bibble," Elina replied, "but . . . maybe we should go home, too."

"I'll ask my mom about Laverna," said Dandelion.

Dandelion flew off for home as Elina and Bibble made their way through the eerily quiet meadow. The sun was just going down when Elina and Bibble reached Peony. Peony was more than a beautiful blossom. She was Elina's home. As Elina drew near, Peony began a lilting song of welcome. Her petals opened to reveal a darling little home.

Inside, Peony's delicate petals formed all the furniture. There was a pillowy bed, a skirted dressing table, and some poufy little chairs. Elina bustled around her tiny home as Bibble floated toward the bed.

"I hope Topaz is all right," Elina said. "Don't you, Bibble? Bibble?"

ZZZZZZ! Bibble was already fast asleep.

Elina laughed. "At least one of us will get a good night's sleep," she said. Peony began to sing again, a soft, lilting melody. "A lullaby," Elina said gratefully. "Peony, you always know just what to do."

As Elina yawned, Peony's petals gently tucked her into bed.

Chapter 2
Elina's Daring Journey

The next morning, Bibble fluttered anxiously above Elina. *"Bleeple, bleeple, blurple!"* she trilled.

Elina slowly opened her eyes. "Why, Bibble, you're right," she said. "Peony usually sings us awake, but she's not singing today!" Elina looked around. It was clear that Peony was not okay.

Her petals were pale and sickly looking.

Everything drooped sadly. With Bibble at her side, Elina headed for the front door. Usually Peony swept it open for her, but today it slowly slumped to the ground. Outside Elina saw how bad things really were. All the flowers in the Magic Meadow looked sick. Elina felt horrified.

"I know, it's awful, and it's everywhere!" Dandelion cried, zipping over to Elina. "Some fairies are having trouble flying. Elina, the pixies were right," Dandelion continued. "My mom told me Topaz is gone!"

"Someone has to do something!" Elina exclaimed. "What will happen to the Magic Meadow? What will happen to Peony?"

"The nearest guardian is Azura, and she's all the way past Fairy Town," Dandelion said. "Forget it. Everyone's too afraid to even go outside."

Elina looked at poor droopy Peony. Then she peered around the Magic Meadow at all the ailing flowers. Finally, she squared her shoulders and faced her friend.

"I think . . ." she said slowly. "Um . . . I think I have to go to Fairy Town."

"You've never even left the Magic Meadow," Dandelion reminded her. "You can't go."

"*Blarp!*" added Bibble.

"It takes hours," Dandelion added, "and that's if you're flying and know exactly

where you're going."

"Brrroooop!" Bibble nodded.

"So I'll be there by nightfall," Elina said absently. "Good."

"Elina!" Dandelion shouted. "You can't go to Fairy Town alone!"

"Oh, I won't be alone," Elina assured her. "I'll be with Bibble."

"Brip, blip, blar-beroop!" Bibble twittered in alarm.

Dandelion and Elina stared at each other. Dandelion could see the determination in her friend's rainbow eyes.

"I'm coming with you!" Dandelion exclaimed.

"Let's do it!" Elina cheered, hugging her

friends tightly. Elina could feel how much Dandelion and Bibble really cared about her, and so they set off together across the Magic Meadow toward Fairy Town.

Chapter 3
Laverna's Potion

If Elina had known how scary the wicked Laverna really was, she might not have been so quick to go find her. Unlike the rest of Fairytopia, Laverna didn't cherish things that were soft and pretty like flowers, or beautiful and sparkly like gems. She lived in the center of an enormous prickly cactus, and she loved to sit on her ugly cactus throne.

The only sparkly thing in Laverna's throne room was the captive Guardian

Fairy, Topaz. The golden gem around her neck was carved in the shape of a butterfly and cast a glowing light around her. In the center of the butterfly gem was a symbol of a diamond within a circle. It matched a similar symbol carved into Laverna's throne. Topaz blinked with dismay as Laverna bragged about her evil plan.

"It won't work, Laverna," Topaz told her.

"The fairies are loyal to the Enchantress. They'll never bow to you."

"Now why didn't I think of that?" Laverna asked mockingly. "Oh wait, I *did* think of that. Fungus!" Laverna's ugly henchmen hurried to do her bidding.

Since they all looked alike, Laverna called them by a single name, Fungus. The creatures were not too bright, so they didn't seem to care. Now they opened large panels in the walls of Laverna's cactus to reveal enormous windows.

Topaz stared in horror. Outside were more arms of the same cactus Laverna had hollowed out to make her creepy home. Some of these had been hollowed out, too, and an oozy green mixture bubbled inside them.

"My potion has the amazing power to weaken every flying creature in Fairytopia," Laverna boasted. "They have no choice but to give in."

Laverna had sent her firebirds out into Fairytopia, each with a vat of green ooze in its talons. As they flew, the gunk hissed down to the ground in a choking green mist. It sickened the plants and weakened the fairies, pixies, and other sprites of Fairytopia.

Topaz hung her head as she realized that Laverna was right.

No one could stop her.

Chapter 4
The Path to Fairy Town

Feeling very tired, Elina, Dandelion, and Bibble trudged to the end of the Magic Meadow, where a high hedgerow loomed above them. Inside it looked cramped and dark. "No wonder I never left the Magic Meadow," Elina ventured weakly. "It's spooky in there."

"*Bippety-bip-bip,*" Bibble trilled.

"Right," Elina agreed, stepping forward into the thicket. "I'm not scared, either."

It was late afternoon by the time they emerged from the hedgerow. Elina and Dandelion found themselves in a vast field of flowers, but not the kind of flowers they were used to in the Magic Meadow. These flowers were enormous and grew wildly in

every direction—along the ground, side-ways, and straight up.

"Where are we?" Elina asked, looking around. "They say that after the hedgerow, fairy wings will guide your way," Elina reminded her friends.

Elina jumped from flower to flower, until suddenly she spotted an unusual purple blossom. It looked like a tunnel, and the petals on either side of the tunnel were shaped just like a pair of fairy wings! Elina knew that she had found the path to Fairy Town. Quickly, they all climbed up and started inside.

The tunnel was roomy enough for Elina to walk while Dandelion and Bibble floated overhead. Its walls glowed blue with the setting sun. Suddenly, Dandelion fell and nearly crashed into Elina!

"Are you okay?" Elina asked.

"It's the flying sickness," Dandelion admitted. "I just need to rest for a second."

"Yes, you do," Elina told her firmly. "And then you need to go home."

"No, no, if I can't fly, I'll walk," Dandelion assured her.

"No, you won't," Elina said. "I'm used to walking, but you're not. Anyway, if you're not home by dark . . ."

"My mom!" Dandelion cried. "You're right, she'll panic."

Elina smiled and took her friend's

hands. "I never would have made it this far without you, Dandelion. Thanks." They hugged before Dandelion headed back out of the tunnel.

Elina and Bibble continued on through the twisting, turning tunnel until they reached an enormous room that seemed to go on forever. It was empty, except for a large fairy hovering near a massive desk. His name was Quill, and he seemed to be waiting for something.

Elina cleared her throat nervously. "Hello?"

"I'm sorry, you need to leave. City Hall is closed," he told them.

Elina and Bibble glanced at each other.

What should they do now?

Then a messenger fairy flew into the room.

"Larkspur!" Quill said quickly. "We have a message that Ruby and Amethyst have been taken. Azura must be told immediately." Larkspur nodded and zoomed off. When Quill looked down again, Elina and Bibble were gone.

They were following Larkspur. As he flew overhead, they raced below him on the ground. On and on he went, until he led them to a glittering blue forest.

The forest actually turned out to be a patch of gigantic azure flowers. In its midst stood a cottage built into the stem of an especially large bloom.

This must be Azura's house, Elina thought.

Unfortunately, the blue cottage was surrounded by flying guards. Crouching low to avoid detection, Elina and Bibble headed toward the nearest window.

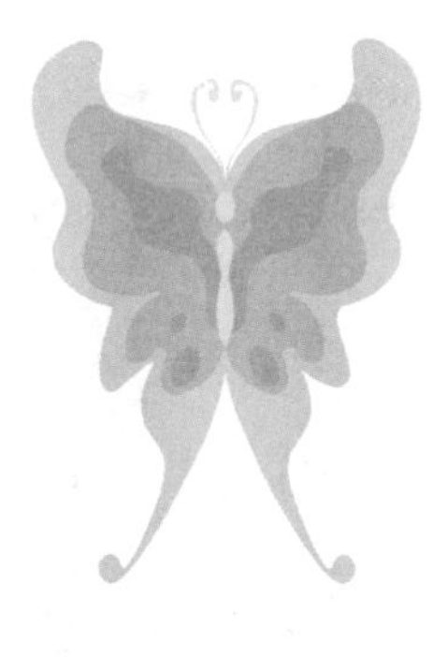

Chapter 5
Azura's Gift

When Elina peered inside, she gasped in astonishment. Like Peony, everything inside was part of the plant, but azure flowers grew inside, too. Loveliest of all was Azura herself as she stood listening to Larkspur. Her gorgeous blue butterfly necklace glinted in the last rays of the setting sun.

Larkspur left, and Azura spoke into one of the flowers along her walls. Her voice seemed to blast right into Elina and

Bibble's hiding place. They jumped in alarm.

"You! Leave immediately before I call my guards!"

Oh, no—Azura thought Elina was an enemy!

Stammering, Elina tried to explain. At first Azura didn't seem to believe her. Finally she went to the window to see them better. When she saw the rainbow shining in Elina's eyes, it was Azura's turn to give a little gasp.

"You'd better come in," she said kindly. Inside, Azura led them to a table elegantly set for eight people. "You must eat. You've had a long journey, and you need nourishment," the Guardian Fairy insisted. "*Bon appétit*."

Bibble started eating, but Elina hesitated. Azura caught her looking at the other place settings.

"Those are for the friends I haven't met yet," she explained.

"How can you have a friend you haven't met?" Elina asked.

"Easy," Azura told her. "I'm sure if I met all of the fairies in Fairytopia, I'd find them delightful and want them as friends. So I keep my table set with extra places to remind myself to do what's right for the friends I have and haven't met."

They finished the delicious dinner and sat back. Elina told Azura about the awful sickness in the Magic Meadow and her journey to Fairy Town. Azura gave Elina a thoughtful look.

"The rainbow in your eyes is a sign," she said. "You're destined for great things, Elina."

"Yeah, right," Elina scoffed. "I don't have wings. I can't even fly like the other fairies. What's great about that?"

"You might be surprised," Azura said softly.

In a dreamy blue bedroom, Azura tucked Bibble into one bed while Elina snuggled into the soft petals of the other. "I always thought the Enchantress's evil twin sister was a myth," Elina said sleepily.

"Oh, no, Laverna is real," Azura assured her. "She's as wicked as our Enchantress is loving, and now all of Fairytopia is in danger. Tomorrow I'll journey to speak with Dahlia, a dryad who lives in the Wildering Wood. She used to follow Laverna, and might know how to stop her. But first I need a favor, Elina."

Azura insisted that Elina wear her guardian necklace for safekeeping. "My trip is dangerous but necessary to keep my friends from harm," Azura said. "That includes the friends I haven't met, too. I'll see you tomorrow before I leave."

Elina was already sleeping as Azura glided out of the room. She didn't hear Azura murmur, "Perhaps."

Chapter 6
Firebirds in Pursuit

Early the next morning, Azura woke Bibble. She gave her a scroll and some important instructions. Bibble was to find a friend of Azura's named Hue and give him the scroll. While Elina slept on, Bibble floated safely out the window.

Azura was not so lucky, however. As she tried to leave, she came face-to-face with three of Laverna's Fungus.

Laverna already had Topaz, Ruby, and

Amethyst. In her throne room, she was explaining her evil plan to them. First she showed them how she had trapped her twin in a sleeping spell.

"Azura, welcome," Laverna sang when Fungus walked in with Azura. "I was just explaining that once I have all seven Guardian Fairies, I will have the full rainbow of powers in the necklaces the Enchantress gave you. Then I will have ALL the power."

When Laverna realized that Azura's blue butterfly was not around her neck, her face grew bright red with fury.

"Wait," Fungus said slowly. "I saw a blue necklace on a little sleeping fairy girl, the one without any wings."

"A fairy without wings?" Laverna screeched. "A fairy without wings won't be affected by my potion. She could ruin everything. Find her now, Fungus! Use every creature at my disposal and bring her to me!"

Meanwhile, Elina was having a strange morning. She woke up all alone in Azura's cottage. The guard fairies had been knocked out and tied up. Azura was gone, and Bibble was nowhere to be found. Elina was sure that Laverna had captured Azura, and just as she began to panic, she heard a familiar voice coming from outside.

"Azura? Azura?" the voice cried. It was Quill! His jaw dropped when he recognized Elina. "You!" he gasped. "What are you doing here, and what happened to these guards?"

"I . . . I—it wasn't me," Elina stuttered as she started to leave.

"Get back here!" Quill yelled angrily.

But Elina was too quick for him. She leaped out the window and onto the nearest flower. Just then an enormous shadow passed over her head. Frightened, she looked up to see Bibble floating next to a giant butterfly!

"I'm Hue," the butterfly said. "Your puffball gave me a note from Azura. Get on

my back and I'll take you wherever you want to go."

Quill was still trying to catch Elina, and as she scrambled onto Hue's back, he managed to grab her. Elina screamed, falling backwards through the air. Hue dove to catch her, and the next thing Elina knew she was perched safely on his back.

"Get back here!" yelled Quill, chasing after them.

But he was no match for Hue's speed. Relieved, Elina told Hue to head for the Wildering Wood. With Azura gone, it was up to Elina to find Dahlia the dryad. Fairytopia must be saved!

Soaring high above Fairytopia on Hue's back, Elina learned what it felt like to really fly. Rivers twined below like shining satin ribbons. The different flower meadows looked like a beautiful patchwork quilt of bright colors. Creatures on the ground became tiny, moving specks.

Before they reached the Wildering Wood, though, Laverna's evil firebirds caught up with them. "Hold on, everybody!" shouted Hue.

Hue began to swoop and dive with the firebirds in hot pursuit. Their sharp, snapping beaks were only inches away. Elina could hardly believe her ears when she heard Hue laughing.

"You think this is funny?" she asked in amazement.

"The odds of our surviving against six firebirds are something like a million to one," Hue explained.

"What's funny about that?" Elina asked, alarmed.

"I love being the one!" Hue yelled. "Yee-haw!" With a burst of speed, he zoomed over a river. Hue followed its twists and turns until suddenly the river ended in a rushing waterfall. With a wild shout, Hue twisted into a steep dive, and they plunged into the misting spray.

Chapter 7
Prince Nalu and the Merpeople

At the foot of the waterfall, turquoise waters lapped in a small, secluded pool. The waterfall formed a glittering backdrop of shifting rainbows as the sun caught in its mist. Three merpeople lounged around the pool, sipping from exotic shells. Two were mermaids, and the last was a merman named Prince Nalu.

Their peaceful sunbathing was rudely interrupted when Hue swooped low over their heads. Their shell drinks flying, the merpeople dove underwater. Prince Nalu surfaced in time to see Hue land in a nearby cave, and angrily, he swam over. He was just about to start hollering at Hue for his carelessness when he caught sight of Elina.

His handsome face broke into a dazzling

smile. "Oh, hi," he said, extending a hand toward Elina. "I'm Nalu." As Elina shook his hand, it was clear that she was just as charmed by Nalu as he was by her.

"Well, I think we gave those firebirds the slip," Hue crowed.

At the mention of firebirds, Prince Nalu peeked outside the cave. The firebirds were circling overhead, spiraling lower and lower. Just then, a firebird dove at the mouth of the protected cave.

Nalu dove underwater and came up with an armload of seaweed. "Eat this, all of you," he ordered. "It will help you breathe underwater."

Elina, Bibble, and Hue quickly ate the slimy

seaweed before diving underwater with Nalu to escape the snapping firebirds. He was right. They *could* breathe underwater!

Silently, Nalu led them through a deep-sea cavern. Its walls were aglow with exotic plants and gorgeous underwater crystal formations. Elina and Nalu traveled side by side, marveling at the amazing scenery. They stayed below as long as they could, but all too soon it was time to surface.

They emerged in a completely different land than the one they had left behind. There were no firebirds in sight. Elina, Bibble, and Hue needed to hurry on to the Wildering Wood, but Elina hated to say good-bye to the charming prince.

"Be safe," Nalu told her, touching her cheek and gazing into her rainbow eyes. "I hope one day we'll meet again." Then he dove underwater and swam away.

Sighing, Elina climbed on Hue's back.

Bibble floated nearby, chirping a sing-song tune.

"I am NOT thinking about kissing him, Bibble!" Elina snapped. Her grin and blush gave her away, though.

Hue decided not to tease her, especially since they really needed to keep moving.

Chapter 8
The Wildering Wood

Soon they were gliding above the Wildering Wood. The awful sickness that overtook the Magic Meadow was happening here, too. The plants looked shriveled. Worse, Hue's smooth flying began to falter. Elina insisted that he land. She knew he had the flying sickness now, and he needed to rest.

Leaving Bibble to care for the butterfly, Elina took off through the trees by herself.

It was dark under the overhanging tree canopy. It wasn't long before Elina worried that she might have gone too far.

"This is crazy," she muttered. She looked at Azura's butterfly pendant and shook her head. "Azura's supposed to be the one seeing Dahlia, not me. She's a Guardian Fairy, and I'm . . . I'm nothing." Elina felt sad and lost. "I don't have a chance," she sighed. As if it heard her, Azura's necklace lit up, and a blue glow filled the forest.

Two happy trolls popped up. They were kind of cute, but also kind of annoying because they only spoke in rhyme. The trolls agreed to lead Elina to Dahlia the dryad, and the fairy followed them. After a long walk, they came to a group of trees that looked just like all the other ailing trees in the forest.

"We're here," said the first happy troll. "Have no fear," added the second.

"But where is here?" Elina cried. "I'm looking for Dahlia the dryad, and there's nothing here but the trees we've seen before!" Azura's necklace burst into light again, shining directly on a nearby tree.

"Azura," a voice said, and a beautiful ghostly spirit floated out from the tree. "I hear your necklace calling." Dahlia stopped when she saw Elina. "You're not Azura!"

Elina explained all that had happened. Dahlia didn't seem eager to help her,

though. The happy trolls beat a hasty retreat, leaving Elina alone with Dahlia.

"I tried to help ten years ago when I realized how wicked Laverna really was," Dahlia said bitterly. "No one would listen, except Azura. Everyone thought I was some kind of spy. Why should I risk my neck for Fairytopia? I don't even know most of those fairies."

"They're the friends you haven't met yet," Elina said simply. "That's what Azura would say. It means you have to do what's right, even if it's not easy. I guess she thought you'd know that. I'm sorry I bothered you." Elina sadly walked away.

Dahlia watched her with a wistful look

on her face. Finally she called out, "Wait. Maybe I can help you."

Elina and Dahlia made their way back to Bibble and Hue. Once they heard what Elina and Dahlia had planned, they wanted to help, too. Trying to sneak up on Laverna and foil her evil plan was dangerous, but everyone wanted to give it their best shot.

"One thing we have going for us is surprise," Dahlia assured them. "Laverna will never expect this ragtag bunch to have the nerve to come after her."

Chapter 9
Laverna's Secret

As the four heroes began their brave journey flying toward Laverna's lair, Dahlia told them what she had learned as a member of Laverna's inner circle. Laverna had created a device that magnified the strength of her royal bloodline. This extra power allowed Laverna to steal the combined powers of the Guardian Fairies' necklaces for herself. If her plan worked, she truly would be unstoppable.

"How does it work?" Elina asked.

"I'm not sure, exactly," Dahlia answered. "She was still working on it when I left. But she always said it had one weakness that made it fragile. She called it the union point."

"What is the union point?" Elina asked.

"I don't know," Dahlia admitted. "I only hope we'll know it when we see it."

Something on the ground caught Dahlia's eye. "There," she told Hue. "Land behind that boulder."

After they landed, they carefully peered over the large rock—and found themselves high above Laverna's lair. It looked like it was a grouping of gigantic, spiky cactus plants.

The largest of these held Laverna's throne room. The smaller plants around it hissed and bubbled with Laverna's foul green potion.

Firebirds wheeled and screeched in the sky. Laverna's Fungus crawled everywhere like giant ants. Dahlia pointed at what looked like a crack in one of the walls. "That's the entrance," she said. "We can't fly there, though. They'd spot us for sure."

Elina knew that if more than one person tried to cross on foot, they'd be too obvious. She had to do this alone. Her friends tried to talk her out of it, but finally they had to agree.

"I have Azura's necklace," Elina reminded them. "I'll find the union point. I promise." Elina hugged each of her friends and headed for the crack in the wall.

It was tricky picking her way among the cactus spines, but they kept her hidden. She had a few close calls with the Fungus, and only got through thanks to her quick thinking and amazing talent for leaping and running. Finally, there was just a small open space between Elina and Laverna's lair.

Nervously she crept into the opening, but then she heard a Fungus shout, and she knew she was in trouble. She tried to keep still, whispering, "Please don't see me," over and over to herself.

A mighty roar filled the air.

It wasn't the screech of a firebird. It wasn't the rumble of a Fungus.

It was Hue, with Dahlia and Bibble on his back! As the butterfly rose into the air, all three hollered as loud as they could. Bibble and Dahlia threw rocks at the Fungus, creating a distraction. Would it work? Could it work?

Not waiting to find out, Elina raced for the entrance.

Chapter 10
The Union Point

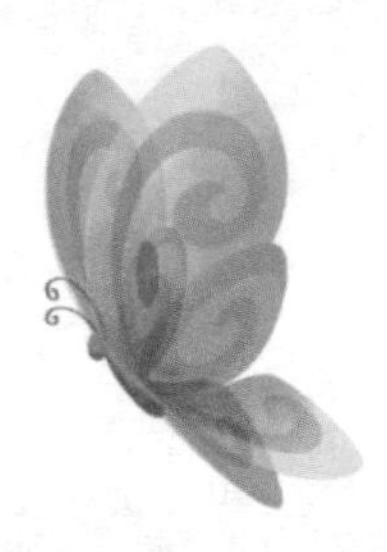

Inside Laverna's throne room, all seven Guardian Fairies were now her captives. Laverna flitted around the chamber. As she considered her plan, the smile on her face was pure evil.

"Now that we're all together, it won't be long before I'll be your new queen," she told the Guardian Fairies smugly.

"Gathering our necklaces won't make you queen," Azura shot back. "You have no way to get at the power inside those gems."

"Oh, don't I?" Laverna asked sweetly. "Why, what's this?" she cried, pretending to pull something from behind Azura's ear. When she opened her hand, a clear diamond-shaped crystal sparkled in it. "This crystal happens to be my family crest," she went on, "from the double throne my sister and I shared when I still ruled part of Fairytopia."

"That was before you revealed your wicked mind and were dethroned, Laverna," Azura reminded her.

"That doesn't matter," Laverna replied. "When placed in just the right spot, the crest will deliver the gems' powers directly to me." She placed the crystal in the center of the symbol carved into her throne.

"Oh, look," Azura said evenly. "Nothing happened."

"Don't worry," Laverna promised. "It will."

For the first time Azura looked worried. Then the gems in the necklaces of the other six Guardian Fairies began to blaze with

brightly colored light.

"The gems feel the presence of their sister," Laverna pointed out. "The wingless fairy must be here. Bring her to me!" she commanded her Fungus.

The Guardian Fairies looked worried, then confused. The Fungus burst in

carrying not Elina but Hue, Bibble, and Dahlia instead.

"Dahlia," Laverna gushed. "Long time, no see. Now I see you're friends with the wingless fairy. How perfect. Where is she, by the way?"

Elina had managed to avoid detection as she stumbled through the dark, narrow halls of Laverna's palace. A blue light shot out of the gloom. It was Azura's necklace, pointing the way again. Elina quickly climbed up a winding staircase.

When she reached the top, she gasped. She was in Laverna's throne room! The Guardian Fairies sat, necklaces glowing, trapped by Laverna's enchanted ropes.

Elina's three friends were similarly tied on the floor nearby.

Laverna floated down from the ceiling and tried to snatch Azura's butterfly gem from Elina's neck. Elina whirled to face Laverna, clutching the precious necklace. Now it was Laverna's turn to step back as she saw the rainbow gleam in Elina's eyes.

"Interesting," she commented. "You have the rainbow in your eyes. Some would say that makes you no ordinary fairy."

"I'm not," Elina told her.

"No, of course not," Laverna crooned. "You're special, like me. But they don't treat you like you're special, do they? Instead they laugh because you're different. I can change all that. Look!"

Now Laverna used her power to create the illusion of black wings sprouting from Elina's shoulders. Elina turned her head this way and that to admire them.

"Wings," she breathed.

Laverna saw Elina weakening. She flew down and took Elina's hands in her own. Her face seemed to shine with kindness and concern. "Together we can have what we've always wanted," Laverna murmured. "I will rule Fairytopia, and you'll have your wings."

Elina blinked, forcing her gaze away from the gorgeous wings. "What about Peony?" she asked. "What about my friends?"

"Everything will be fine," Laverna

vowed. "Just put the necklace around Azura's neck, and you'll see."

Elina moved dreamily toward the couch. Azura remained still, her facial expression neutral. As Elina drew closer, the blue light began to arc through the air, joining the lights from the other Guardian Fairies' necklaces in a beautiful rainbow.

Laverna danced in the rainbow light. "Yes, Elina," she urged. "You're so close to everything you've ever wanted. Your little world will be perfect soon."

Trancelike, Elina continued. Something bright flared above her and she looked up. One of Laverna's mirrors reflected the diamond crest in Laverna's throne. Elina could see the rainbow lights gathered into its point.

"The union point," she whispered. Wheeling on Laverna, she suddenly shouted, "My world is not so little, Laverna!" She hurled Azura's necklace across the room, directly at the diamond crest. With a loud *CRACK*, the clear crystal shattered.

"NOOOOO!" Laverna screeched as the rainbow lights began zooming back into the necklaces. Then the lights bounced back, brighter than before, to wrap Laverna in a swirl of rainbow glow. Laverna rose in the air, imprisoned in the whirling rainbow. Higher and higher she twirled, until the rainbow lights suddenly turned black and disappeared, taking Laverna with them.

Chapter 11
The Gift of the Enchantress

When Elina returned to the Magic Meadow, it was bright and healthy again. Peony seemed more beautiful than ever, and Hue took to hovering near the giant blossom.

Dandelion wasted no time hurrying over. Elina was overjoyed to be with all of her friends again, both new and old. "So, what shall we do today?" Elina asked them.

Just then a rainbow glow fell over the

meadow. Swirling colors surrounded a lovely figure. Though she looked very much like Laverna, her face was kind and loving. Goodness shone from her eyes. It was the Enchantress!

"I've come to thank you," she told them. "Without your bravery and your willingness to sacrifice for others, Fairytopia might have been lost. You have earned a great gift, Elina."

"Thank you," Elina said politely. "But honestly, I've already been given the greatest gift of all. I used to think I was useless, because I wasn't like all the other fairies. Now I know that's not true. I am different, but that's okay . . . better than

okay, really. Best of all, I have amazing friends who love me just the way I am."

"I'm glad," the Enchantress told her, smiling. "You are destined for great things, Elina." Then she kissed Elina on both cheeks and disappeared in a rainbow swirl.

Elina's friends stared. Two rainbow-colored kisses adorned Elina's face. As they watched, the marks began to swirl and grow larger. Finally they slid off Elina's face to land on her back. They had become magnificent, glowing wings.

Elina looked dazzled until Hue broke her trance. "Elina," he said, "you have wings!"

"I do?" Elina breathed. "I do!" she shouted. Slowly at first, then faster, Elina

flew into the air. Scooping Bibble into her arms, she soared above Peony. Her friends Hue and Dandelion flew up to join her.

As a glorious rainbow spread its colors over the Magic Meadow, the friends celebrated.

Life was back to normal again.

Actually, it was even better than normal. It was fantastic!

And it was only going to keep getting better.